Hello, Bicycle!

by Ella Boyd   illustrated **by Daniel Griffo**

Marshall Cavendish Children

Text copyright © 2011 by Ella Boyd
Illustrations by Daniel Griffo
Illustrations copyright © 2011 by Marshall Cavendish Corporation

Marshall Cavendish Corporation
99 White Plains Road
Tarrytown, NY 10591
www.marshallcavendish.us/kids

Pinwheel Books

Library of Congress Cataloging-in-Publication Data
Boyd, Ella.
Hello, bicycle / by Ella Boyd ; illustrated by Daniel Griffo.
— 1st Marshall Cavendish Pinwheel Books ed.
p. cm.
Summary: A child has an exciting ride on a new bicycle.
ISBN 978-0-7614-5964-4 (hardcover)
— ISBN 978-0-7614-6076-3 (ebook)
[1. Stories in rhyme. 2. Bicycles and bicycling—Fiction.] I.
Griffo, Daniel, ill. II. Title.
PZ8.3.B6884He 2011   [E]—dc22   2011000032

The illustrations are rendered in Photoshop.
Book design by Vera Soki
Editor: Marilyn Brigham

Printed in Malaysia (T)
First Marshall Cavendish Pinwheel Books edition, 2011
10 9 8 7 6 5 4 3 2 1

To my daughter, son, granddaughter, and grandpuppies. Woof!
—E. B.

For my wife, Elba, and my little son, Benjamin
—D. G.

BYE, BYE, BLUE.
Hello, Red!
Shiny paint.
Smokin' tread.

Climb the seat.
Twist the bars.
Helmet's on.
Check for cars.

Pedal's up.
Dad's in view.
Ready, start—coming through!

Down the hill I *bump, bump, bump.*
Feel it on my rump, rump, rump.

Miss the rock.
Skim the hole.
Squish the hose.
Dodge the pole.

Reach a fence—
dog won't stay.
Hear a bark.
Speed away!

Next house down,
girls can't skate.
Steer around,
doing great!

Up ahead,
hill looks high.
I'm not scared.
Gotta try!

My little heart goes *thump, thump, thump,*
when I make the jump . . . *bump, rump.*

WELL DONE, RED!

We made Dad grin.

Now let's make him smile again!